MERRY CHRISTMAS, PEANUT!

Terry Border

PHILOMEL BOOKS

PHILOMEL BOOKS
an imprint of Penguin Random House LLC
375 Hudson Street
New York, NY 10014

Philomel Books is a registered trademark of Penguin Random House LLC.

Library of Congress Cataloging-in-Publication Data is available upon request.
Manufactured in China by R R Donnelley Asia Printing Solutions Ltd.
ISBN 9780399176210
1 3 5 7 9 10 8 6 4 2

Edited by Jill Santopolo.
Design by Ellice M. Lee.
Text set in Hank BT.

The art was done by manipulating and photographing three-dimensional objects.
Endpaper art copyright © Marinka Alisen/Shutterstock

To my mother,
who was, and still is,
always a believer
and a helper.

It was Christmas Day, and Peanut and his parents were on their way to his grandmother's house for dinner.

Christmas made Peanut happier than anyone he knew. He was nuts about it! And he couldn't wait to see his grandma.

But the ride was taking forever! At first, Peanut thought it was a traffic jam, but then he saw it was a traffic *jelly*.

Peanut wasn't worried,
though. They still had *lots* of
time to get to his grandma's.

Once the car got unstuck, Peanut saw his friend the baker looking very sad. So he asked his parents to stop.

"What's wrong?" Peanut asked.

"Now I can't make my famous jelly doughnuts!" the baker said.

Peanut knew just what to do.

"Don't be sad! I'll cheer you up! I'm the Merry Christmas Nut!" said Peanut. "Come with us to my grandma's house!"

The baker hopped right in.

But then they got to the bridge—and it was broken!

Peanut wasn't worried, though. They still had time to get to his grandma's.

They walked along the riverbank and found a sailor who could help.

As the sailor steered the boat, she seemed unhappy.

"What's wrong?" Peanut asked.

"I don't have any family nearby to visit for Christmas," she said.

Peanut knew just what to do.

"Don't be sad! I'll cheer you up! I'm the Merry Christmas Nut!" said Peanut. "Come with us to my grandma's house!"

"That sounds nice!" said the sailor. So she parked her boat and joined the group.

Once back on land, they had to pass through a forest. Peanut finally started to get worried. There wasn't much time left, and they had to get to his grandmother's for dinner!

Then they met a lumberjack who was looking sad.
"What's wrong?" said Peanut.
"My ax broke while I was chopping down
my Christmas tree!" he said.
Peanut knew just what to do.

"Don't be sad! I'll cheer you up! I'm the Merry Christmas Nut!" said Peanut very quickly. He was in a rush now, trying to get to his grandma's. But he knew she always had a beautiful Christmas tree, so he invited the lumberjack along.

The lumberjack took his lantern and joined the group.

As they walked, they laughed and talked.

But then it started to snow! Just a few flakes fell at first. But before long, snow had completely hidden the path—the only one that led out of the dark forest.

Now Peanut was *really* worried. There was no time left!

And he had to get to his grandmother's house for dinner.
"Don't be sad! We'll cheer you up! You're the Merry
Christmas Nut!" said his parents and his friends.
But Peanut could not be cheered up.
And his parents didn't know what to do.

"I know," said the baker. "I can use my spatula as a shovel!"

"I know," said the sailor. "I can use my spyglass to find the road!"

"I know," said the lumberjack. "I can use my lantern to light the way."

The friends shoveled snow and looked for the road and lit the way, and they finally found the path again. But they needed to move faster. They were going to be late for dinner, and there was so much snow!

Peanut had an idea. "We need to make snow angels!"

"I know you're the Merry Christmas Nut," said the lumberjack, "but snow angels? Now?"

"Trust me," said Peanut.

So each of them lay down and moved the snow with their arms and legs, which uncovered the path below!

Everyone was so excited!

"We aren't sad! You cheered us up! You're the Merry Christmas Nut!" said Peanut's friends.

Smiling, Peanut led his friends and his parents to his grandmother's for dinner.

"Merry Christmas, Peanut!"
Grandma said as she opened the door.

"Merry Christmas, Grandma!" Peanut
said. "It's been quite a day!"

Peanut introduced his new friends
to her, and everyone sat down to a huge
Christmas dinner (with jelly doughnuts
for dessert!).

The baker had doughnuts.
The sailor had a family. And the
lumberjack had a beautiful, beautiful
Christmas tree. Everyone was happy.
Except Grandma, who was worried
that some of her guests might
have to leave early because it was
snowing again.

But Peanut knew just what to do.
"Don't be sad! I'll cheer you up!
I'm the Merry Christmas Nut!"
Peanut said.

And so he asked his friends
if they would like to stay
the night.

Of course, *everyone* stayed. Wouldn't you?
And they stayed and played the next day, too.